My Worst Headache

RENATO MALAYBA

My Worst Headache
Copyright © 2024 by Renato Malayba

All rights reserved. No part of this
publication may be reproduced, distributed,
or transmitted in any form or by any means,
including photocopying, recording, or
other electronic or mechanical methods,
without the prior written permission of
the author, except in the case of brief
quotations embodied in critical reviews
and certain other non-commercial
uses permitted by copyright law.

Tellwell Talent
www.tellwell.ca

ISBN
978-0-2288-7262-7 (Paperback)

TABLE OF CONTENTS

High School Days 1

Market 13

The Mischievous Son 20

The Indifferent Husband 27

The Gin 37

The Wake 45

Brawl in the Wake 53

Jail 58

The Revelation 65

The Stroke 70

High School Days

*I*n their sophomore years, Suz served as the platoon leader in Cadet Army Training (CAT) and was a member of the Student Body Organization (SBO). She had a boyfriend after finishing school and they eventually tied the knot a few years later.

One afternoon, Kring visited Suz's parents' house. Their residence stood as an elevated bungalow, adorned with two wide windows overlooking the roadside, and featured unpainted, somewhat weathered six-stepped stairs. Ascending to their balcony, a subtle sound accompanied each step, creating a quiet prelude to the scenes awaiting discovery.

As Kring reached the summit, she encountered Suz's father, Mr. Cielo. Slender, with a crown of gray hair, he sat in his rocking chair, enveloped in the muted glow of the television's flickering light. His solitude hinted at a moment of personal reflection.

"Hello, Mr. Cielo, how are you doing?" Kring ventured.

Mr. Cielo came to the door, "Who is it?", his eyes squinting from the sun coming through the door.

"Mr. Cielo, it's me, Kring."

"O wow! Come inside, please. Please bear with the scattered items on our couches," the surprise very evident in Mr. Cielo's voice.

Acknowledging the request, Kring proceeded to tidy up the disarray, picking up clothes strewn across a seat and carefully placing them on one side.

"Have a seat, please, on that comfortable chair" Mr. Cielo warmly suggested.

"Thank you, sir."

As Kring settled into the designated chair, Mr. Cielo, with a glint of nostalgia, remarked, "It has been several years since we last saw each other."

"Yes, sir. How are you, sir?" Kring inquired, delving beyond the surface.

"I am old now, and my time companions these days are Mr. Hypertension and Prof.

Diabetes," he chuckled, revealing the passage of etched upon his features.

"Do you consistently follow your prescribed medication routine?"

"Hmm... not always, you know. The prices are exorbitant, and procuring funds has become an arduous task,"

"You're right, sir."

"Your friend Suz, she causes more than a mere headache. Eloping with her high school boyfriend, she has become the source of my woes. Are you familiar with the tricycle driver sporting long, wavy hair? He resides just two blocks away from us."

"Is he the one consistently engaged in a drinking spree on the street corner?"

"Yes, Kring, that's him!"

"I know him. Let me recall his name. Hmmm... His name is at the tip of my tongue... Ah, gotcha! He is Romel."

"Your memory is truly commendable... the ability to recall a name just like that. My daughter, she's expecting now. The frequent visits and pleas for money have become a routine. Her boyfriend avoids coming here, as I harbor resentment towards him. It's a perpetual source of my escalating blood pressure."

"I'm sorry to hear that, sir."

"I apologize for burdening you with our problems.

Well, do you fancy some coffee or a bite to eat? There are some foods on the table, covered with a small blue basin," Mr. Cielo offered.

"My stomach is still satiated, sir. I've just had a meal at home."

"Alright. When you feel hungry, you know where the food is. You know, I'm curious about Suz's current residence. Any idea about the squatter area approximately two kilometers from here?"

"Yes, sir! I'm familiar with that place."

"Just a second. Can you see that big photo album under the center table?"

"Yes, sir. Do you want me to get it?"

"Okay! Take that out, and the address is written on the piece of paper inserted there."

"Oh! It's here, sir! I'll type in the address on my mobile phone. I'll visit her sometime next week, sir."

"I know you really miss your childhood friendship with my daughter."

The first room door creaked open, and Mrs. Leila emerged, yawning and stretching her arms.

"Oh, my goodness, we have a visitor! I'm sorry our home is a mess!"

She walks towards her husband and taps his right shoulder. "Why didn't you offer her coffee or any food?" Mrs. Leila asked angrily.

"I told her to help herself to get some food on the table, but she said she's full. Kring is like family,"

Mr. Cielo replied in a slightly raised voice. He suddenly stood up and went to his room.

Kring also stood up and asked to leave.

"Kring? Is that you now? It's been so long!", Mrs. Leila rushed to hug her.

"Stay in your seat. You know, we're getting old, and we are an empty nest. This is just what we call a sweet quarrel with my husband. How is everything in your life now, Kring?"

"I also have kids now, and they've all grown up. I work as a freelance laundrywoman," Kring replied.

"Not a permanent job, right?"

"Yes, ma'am!"

"Do you have daily customers?"

"No, I have three to four customers a week."

"Uh! It's not enough to support your family."

"My kids earn a bit from their jobs."

"Okay, good! What is your husband doing?"

"He is my big headache, ma'am. He earns from his part-time job as a mason and helper in construction.

He just gives me a portion of his salary. Do you know where he puts the rest of his money, Mrs. Leila?"

"Where?"

"On his drinking habit with friends. And most of all, on his cockfight betting and illegal lottery game addiction."

"What a life you are enduring now, Kring!", Mrs. Leila said with a frown.

"Yes, it is true, ma'am! Life is hard, but I keep on fighting," Kring said with her eyes moist.

"Everything will be alright," said Mrs. Leila as she held Kring's hands. "What if you come with me as a sidewalk vendor in the market? You will earn extra."

"How is that?", asked Kring.

"We'll be street vendors. Most of the time there are vacant spaces. All we have to do is go there as early as possible."

"I mean, where do I get my vegetables to sell?"

"We must go there early and wait for the middlemen who drop the fresh veggies directly from the farmers."

"How about the fee for the spot?"

"We are lucky if the city ticketers do not roam around. It will be our bonus."

"Really?"

"Yes! Ha... ha..!" They both laughed heartily. Their voices echoed so loudly that even the people walking by the streets caught a glimpse of their lively conversation. The dogs nearby growled and barked, as if joining in on the infectious laughter.

Mr. Cielo emerged from the room.

"Will you talk silently? I am napping, and you both are disturbing me," said Mrs. Leila's husband frantically.

"Okay, okay! Go back to your room. This is not an every-minute, everyday, nor every-year chat," his wife irritably replied.

"Let us return to our lively conversation. Sorry for Mr. Cielo's reaction. We engage in these heated arguments almost every day. He sometimes gives me a headache."

"Sorry to hear that, ma'am!"

"Again! Do you like coffee?"

"No, ma'am, thank you!"

"You know, Kring! You should be very careful in our environment now."

"Why do you say that?" I asked.

"Do you watch the daily news?"

"Oh! We do not have a television."

"Listen, Kring! Do you know what happened to the store staff one block away from here?"

"No! What?"

"The bread store on our corner was robbed by an unidentified assailant. The intruder entered the store and grabbed the owner with a pointed knife on his neck. But the owner refused to give the money in his cash machine; he was stabbed in his abdomen. He was found dead laying on the floor by his wife. It happened after lunchtime."

"The burglars nowadays attack at any time of the day."

"Yes, you are right, Kring."

"What happened to the case?"

"It is still under police investigation. Nobody witnessed the incident. And if there is, they will just remain silent because of fear. Based on the news I heard, it happened only within 5 minutes. Even the wife did not hear the commotion."

"It's fast," said Kring.

"It is true! More and more people nowadays are desperate for money. One thing more!" Mrs. Leila paused for a while and held her forehead.

"Are you alright, ma'am?" said Kring emphatically.

"This is nothing. I am experiencing this headache sometimes."

"Have you consulted your doctor?"

"I do not have extra money to consult a doctor. This will be gone. Don't worry! Where did I stop?"

"You stopped at 'one thing more,'" Kring said.

"Oh yeah! One thing more..."

Mrs. Leila gently shook her head while massaging her forehead for a few seconds. She closed her eyes for a moment then continued, "One thing more, Kring. Be smart and vigilant in the market. There are several swindlers."

"How do they do it?" Kring reacted briskly, her eyes widening.

"I will tell you when we are already in the market." Mrs. Leila stood.

"Do you want a cup of coffee? Don't be shy, young lady. This is free."

"I won't say no now, ma'am. After this, I'll be going home. My kids are waiting for me. I have to prepare food for them."

"Ok, Kring! When do you want to start in the market with me?"

"Sunday."

"Alright! Let's do it!"

They both clinked their coffee cups, sealing their newfound partnership with a shared moment of warmth.

MARKET

It was a bustling Sunday at the market, a throng of shoppers rushing to get their fresh produce and meat for the traditional Sunday meal get-together. The two-way street groaned under the weight of traffic, as cars, jeeps, and trucks navigated through bumper-to-bumper chaos. Street vendors orchestrated a lively symphony of commerce, their voices rising above the urban clamor. The street appeared to culminate in both left and right directions, with vendors occupying every available space – some perched on small chairs, while others squatted behind mini tables, adorned with circular baskets or large basins.

For Kring, this marked her debut as a peddler. Her basin displayed an array of fresh produce – cabbages, bokchoys, squash, gourds, tomatoes, and moringa leaves.

Seated to her left, Mrs. Leila, an indefatigable vendor, energetically hailed potential buyers.

"Hey madam! Beautiful lady! Please buy some of my veggies so that I can go home early. They are fresh and affordable."

"Oh, you know what? Since you are a gorgeous young lady, I will give you a discount. You make my day very good! It is only ₱25/kilo."

"Ok! I will buy all your bokchoy."

"Thank you! Thank you! You are my angel today!" Mrs. Leila joyfully packed the vegetables in a bag and handed it to the lady.

"Here, Miss lovely lady!"

"Thank you!" the buyer expressed gratitude.

"You are welcome," Mrs. Leila beamed.

While counting her earnings, Mrs. Leila observed Mike and Jeff approaching Kring. Swiftly, she stashed the money in her apron and rose from her seat.

Kring, immersed in a pocketbook, was jolted when someone tapped her basin, causing it to teeter.

"What do you want?" she retorted; her anger evident as she stood up. Setting down her eyeglasses with a colorful lace, she allowed them to dangle around her neck. Adjusting her wrinkled shirt and old, flowing skirt, she combed her hair with her right fingers, imparting a playful curl.

"Oh! It's you, macho man. Next time, tap my shoulder and not my basin," she quipped, charmingly catching them off guard.

"I do not like your face, Miss! I want the money! Your share!"

"Ah! Well... I do not have sales yet."

Jeff approached Kring and firmly grasped her right arm.

"Hey! We come here for your daily share."

"Relax! My arm hurts! Don't touch me!"

Jeff released her arm. Mrs. Leila rushed to Kring.

"What is happening here?", asked Mrs. Leila.

"Don't interrupt! Mind your own business!" Mike exclaimed.

"I have the authority to intervene. She is my friend. She is just new here," Mrs. Leila replied.

"Just stay away, and you'll not be hurt!" said Mike furiously.

"Alright!" Mrs. Leila moved one step backward calmly. Other people and vendors were stunned, merely observing the tense confrontation.

"When would you give the money?" asked Jeff.

"Can you give me a free day, macho men? This is my first day here."

"There is no exemption. New and old are the same. So, when?" asked Mike.

"Maybe tomorrow. Just give me more time today to sell all my veggies," said Kring with a slightly intimidating expression.

"Ok! Tomorrow!" Jeff declared as he pointed his finger towards Kring. The tension lingered, leaving the onlookers in hushed amazement.

Both Jeff and Mike walked away, leaving a heightened atmosphere behind. Mrs. Leila approached Kring, concern etched across her face.

"Are you alright? Those are bastards! They don't work legally and fairly."

"Psst...! They might hear you."

"Let us sit first," said Mrs. Leila. "Here is another monobloc chair. Sit beside me."

"You know, Mrs. Leila? Can I call you Leila instead of using Mrs? You are twenty years older than me, and you are making yourself look more aged by using Mrs. I will make you younger and more beautiful than me."

"Really? I like it! This is why you are my daughter's best friend, and you'll become my best friend forever. See! I am older than you, but I can still adapt to the millennial acronym. Ha..ha..!!"

"Hey! Two ladies are at your veggie stand."

"Ok! I will go back to my place," said Kring.

"Hi, beautiful girls! Will you buy some of my vegetables?" said Kring with excitement.

"Yes! Please give us one kilo each of your veggies."

"Ok, ma'am! Please select and put them in the weighing scale. Would you like plastic bags?"

"No! We have our own bag. How much?"

"Just a minute. I will get my calculator. The total is two hundred twelve pesos."

"What is your name?" the customer asked politely.

"Kring, ma'am!"

"Ok! Here is ₱220. You can keep the change," one lady said.

"Yes, because you called us beautiful girls," the other lady grinned.

"Thank you, gorgeous girls!" Kring chuckled, the tension from the earlier scene momentarily forgotten in the warmth of this new interaction.

"Come again!"

"Yes, we will."

Leila returns to Kring.

"Congratulations! You've truly mastered the art of charming customers. That was the best performance I've observed from you while you were talking to the ladies. I like it!"

"It's still my pinky level, Leila. Hahaha!" Leila laughed with her.

"I have a few remaining veggies to sell, Leila. I think I have to offer them at low prices so that I can go home. It's 6:00 PM now, and I need to cook food at home."

The Mischievous Son

"Joey! Joey, where are you?" Kring's urgent plea echoed through the treehouse. The call hung in the air, unanswered, as if the very essence of the wooden sanctuary had absorbed the sound, leaving only the rustle of leaves and the distant murmur of life beyond.

Lying on a diminutive bed within the cozy quarters, Joey remained indifferent to his mother's plea – his gaze fixated on the open window, hands cradling his head, lost in contemplation. An unsettling stillness enveloped him, an enigmatic aura rendering him inscrutable, almost distant.

The treehouse, a resilient testament to the craftsmanship of father and son, stood defiant against the onslaught of time and weather. A mere 1.5 x 1.5 square meters, it encapsulated a history of shared endeavors—constructions undertaken amidst laughter, shouts, and the rawness of familial bonds.

"I was handing up pieces of wood to my father as we fixed this house," Joey murmured to the solitude around him. Memories unfolded like the pages of an old photo album; each recollection etched in the grain of the wood beneath him.

"We looked like brothers during those days."

His mind meandered back to a close call; a falling hammer suspended in time.

"Joey, look out!"

The words, once urgent, lingered in the air, a reminder of fleeting moments and near misses. Yet, amidst the close calls, the treehouse stood resilient, a silent witness to their shared history.

"I don't want to go down," Joey muttered to himself, a whisper carried away by the wind.

The outside world, with its demands and expectations, seemed distant and uninviting. The mere thought of exposing himself to the scrutiny of others invoked a silent resistance within him.

As the chorus of his mother's calls persisted, Joey's detachment deepened.

"I don't want to go down," he reiterated, a plea for solace within the sanctuary of his thoughts.

A distant murmur reached his ears—the voices of two approaching figures. Curiosity sparked, and Joey's eyes found their way to a discreet peephole in the wall.

"Gosh!" he exclaimed under his breath, recognizing the approaching silhouettes of Russel and Molly.

In the dance of shadows and secrecy, the quiet treehouse became a haven for clandestine observations.

Unseen and unheard, Joey observed the world unfold beyond the protective embrace of the sturdy wooden walls. The eavesdropping leaves and the creaks of the tree branches bore witness to a silent drama, unraveling in the intimate confines of the resilient treehouse.

They went to the house, staying near the closed gate, a feeling of excitement in the air. Molly called out for Joey, her voice echoing in the quiet. Russel, standing beside her, thought about the situation.

"Maybe he's not here," he said, uncertain like a faint wisp of smoke in his words.

Suddenly, Kring appeared at the door, watchful and sharp.

"Hey! Who are you?" she asked, like a guard facing intruders at night.

Molly, not bothered by the intensity, quickly replied, "We're friends of Joey."

"Is he there?" Molly asked, concern on her face.

Kring's shrug signaled Joey's absence.

"He's not here. I've been looking for him since this morning."

"Okay, ma'am! Please tell him we want to talk to him," Molly requested politely, bringing a bit of courtesy to the tense moment.

"Okay!" Kring agreed with a nod, an understanding like a pact before she went back to the house.

Meanwhile, Joey stayed in the treehouse, lost in his thoughts. Going back to bed, he continued thinking, his face marked with memories like ancient writings.

"I know Russel well," he thought, his words carried away by the evening breeze, like whispers among ghosts.

"I was surprised why he did that to me. He was my best friend since 2nd grade.

His mind drifted back to their shared adventures—climbing trees, eating fruits, and narrowly escaping dogs. Moments etched in the sacred history of their friendship.

The memories unfolded, leading him to a perilous moment by the lake.

"Russel saved my life," Joey acknowledged, gratitude lingering in his memories.

The story shifted to a less ideal memory—a tale of paternal discipline and misunderstanding. Wet shorts led to accusations, and his father's stern hand left its mark.

"Well, past is past," Joey sighed, a recognition of irreversible moments.

With the dark approaching and mosquitoes buzzing, he descended from his perch for food.

Entering the house, Joey caught his mother's attention.

"Where have you been?" Kring asked, concern on her face like a weathered sculpture.

His response, delivered with anger, added tension, "It's none of your business!"

The air thickened as he found his waiting meal.

Silence filled the room as he ascended back to the treehouse, food in hand. Kring, grappling with her emotions, retreated to her room. The night unfolded, weaving a tale of secrecy, unresolved tensions, and untold stories that cast shadows on their shared history.

THE INDIFFERENT HUSBAND

As Kring's solitary journey homeward unfolded, the echoes of Leila's excitement lingered in her mind. Amidst the urban bustle, she replayed the animated conversation with Leila, the air thick with Leila's fervor for an upcoming birthday celebration.

"Let's attend the birthday party of one of my cousins next week," Leila bubbled with enthusiasm, encouraging Kring to bring not only herself but also her husband, Jose, and their teenagers along.

Kring, however, couldn't suppress a smile as she quickened her pace, traversing the familiar path. Silently conversing with herself, she chuckled at the mental image of her family being referred to as "heavy" companions. Leila probed further, seeking reasons behind Kring's reluctance.

"Why not?" Leila inquired.

Kring, still smiling, replied, "They are heavy," a quirky remark that genuinely amused Leila—a rare sight for Kring, witnessing her friend finding genuine humor in her corny joke.

The moment, however, quickly transitioned into a more serious tone as Kring pledged to approach her family about the invitation. A sudden disclosure unfurled as Kring admitted that her husband, Jose, stood as a formidable thorn in her life, a relentless source of headaches.

"Don't mind it. Any problem can be patched up," Leila reassured, her words echoing as the last fragments of their conversation.

Amidst the dichotomy of Leila's buoyancy and Kring's domestic struggles, Kring grappled with the concept of enjoyment. How could she revel in life when her familial existence was tumultuous? Leila's parting words, urging the prioritization of pleasure, reverberated in her thoughts, posing a challenging paradox.

With a resigned sigh, Kring resumed her journey, the woven rattan basket securely tucked under her right arm. Encounters with neighbors punctuated her route, and Luz, in particular, sought her attention.

A tap on the shoulder and a revelation: Luz had spotted Jose at Beth's variety store, engaged in yet another bout of revelry with his cronies.

"Really?" Kring responded, gratitude threading through her voice.

Luz affirmed, prompting Kring to redirect her path toward the store, determination fueling her strides.

The weight of her burdens mirrored in the load she carried, but she pressed on, driven by an unsettling realization.

"My husband does not care about his family," Kring muttered to herself, each step a testament to the internal conflict she bore. As the distant voices of the group became louder, Jose's unmistakable tone among them, Kring braced herself for the impending confrontation.

The tableau unfolded at Beth's variety store: the wooden bench, the clink of glass, the resonance of laughter, and Jose's voice blending with the chorus. Two bottles of gin and a modest plate of peanuts adorned the table—a tableau of escapism that heightened Kring's resolve to confront the dissonance within her domestic realm.

In the evening shadows, Gerard, a guitarist from a local band, played his guitar with friends. Kring, silently watching from afar, joined the scene unnoticed.

"Hey, Jose!" Kring's voice cut through, breaking the music. It was past 6 o'clock, and she confronted her husband about neglecting their home.

"Why are you still here? You haven't cooked supper! We have no food, and the kids are on their own. Go home and make supper for me!" Kring's words collided with the careless atmosphere.

"What food?" Jose slurred, clearly affected by alcohol. "We don't have any. The kids can handle it."

"Go home, my love," Kring pleaded, desperation in her voice. "If you love me, go home!" But Gerard mockingly dismissed her plea.

"Yes! Go home! We're having fun," Gerard said, ignoring the family turmoil.

"Stop calling me 'my love'; it's a lie! If you love me, go home! And you, Gerard, don't meddle!" Kring struggled to maintain his composure, teetering on the brink of confrontation. Laughter, filled with sarcasm, echoed from Jose and his friends.

Kring's face turned red, fists clenched in frustration. "You're all stupid!" she declared, a lone voice against the noise.

"Do you even know, Jose, that I've been in the market selling vegetables for our family?" Her revelation hung in the air, a contrast to the revelry. Jose, avoiding her gaze, found solace in a bottle of gin.

"Go home before I hit you!" Kring's plea became a demand. A sudden headache hit her, and she massaged her temples. Without a word, she picked up her basket and left.

"Don't you help your wife back home?" Gerard reproached Jose.

"She's not a child; she knows the way," Jose replied casually. "Let's continue our drinking and singing."

As Kring disappeared, the echoes of indifference lingered, a dissonant melody accompanying the ongoing revelry in the dimly lit space.

"Why did I marry this lazy and good-for-nothing person?" Kring's words echoed in her mind as she walked home, a heavy heart burdened with regret. Tears streamed down her face, and with each step, her frustration grew.

Reaching their modest house, Kring swung open the creaky bamboo gate, and it slammed shut behind her. Their two dogs, tails wagging in excitement, rushed towards her.

"Get away from me!" she snapped, kicking one of the dogs away. "Is John here?" she asked the other dog, marching towards the front door.

Upon entering, she was greeted by the sight of her daughter Jasmin in a corner, sitting in a chair. Kring's demeanor softened as she addressed her daughter. "Ooh la la! You are here. Who are you with? Where are your brothers?"

Jasmin stood up, kissing her mom's hand before helping her to the couch.

"Did you prepare food?"

"Only rice, Mom," Jasmin replied.

"Okay, let's start the dish," Kring said, rising from the couch. "Aaaaww...!

"Are you alright, Mom?" Jasmin inquired.

"My head and back are aching," Kring confessed.

"Just be seated, Mom," Jasmin pleaded, a look of concern obviously seen on her face.

"No! You have to help me and cook fast. I am very hungry," Kring insisted. "Get the big can of sardines from the lowest drawer of that cupboard in the corner on the left side."

"Okay, Mom!"

"Open it, and I will gather some camote tops in our backyard."

After a few minutes, Jasmin called out, "Where is the can of sardines?"

"Use your eyes and not your mouth!" Kring retorted.

"Mom! Jay is here!"

"Okay. Tell your brother to help me here! Where have you been, Jay?"

"From my friends, Mom. I will go to the other side to gather some camote tops," Jay suggested. Kring approved.

After several minutes, Kring called Jay, "I think this is enough. I gathered a basin of leaves plus your collected ones, they should be good. Let's go inside now."

As they started preparing the meal, Joey arrived, announcing his presence. "Hello, everyone! Nice meal!

Come here, brother! Let us eat now!" Kring invited him.

While dining, Kring brought up the idea of attending Mr. Luz's cousin's birthday party. Joey and Jay declined, but Jasmin eagerly expressed her interest.

"It is only you, Jasmin, who will go with me. Okay! We'll go to the party next week. I will go to bed now. I am very tired. I want my body ache to be gone."

"Before I forget…clean the dishes, okay?" she instructed Jasmin and Jay.

"Yes, Mom!" they chorused obediently as Kring retreated to rest, leaving behind the dishes that bore the warmth of a simple family meal.

THE GIN

Jose arrived at around 9PM, unlocking the door to their home with weariness etched across his movements. Navigating through the dimly lit space, he made his way straight to the dining area, swaying slightly, his fatigue palpable. In his absentminded state, he overlooked turning on the lights, allowing shadows to cascade and veil the room.

In search of solace or perhaps an escape, he fumbled through the covered shelves, initially seeking soy sauce or fish sauce. A sudden realization brought a glimmer of comfort.

"Oh! There are gins here," he murmured to himself.

Selecting a bottle of fish sauce, he moved towards the wooden long bench chair, intending to find solace in the embrace of the familiar.

Unexpectedly, fate intervened as he tripped and stumbled, the unforgiving corner of a wooden center table meeting his forehead with an audible thud. A small rivulet of blood emerged from the minor wound as he crumpled onto the floor, unconscious and prone.

The unfolding scene played out in stark contrast to the quietude of the night, a silent drama that would only be discovered with the dawn. Meanwhile, Kring, undisturbed by the nocturnal events, slept through the night, unaware of the unforeseen turn of events.

At around 4 AM, Kring stirred from her slumber. Rubbing the sleep from her eyes and grappling with grogginess, she sat on the edge of the bed, stretching her arms as the morning light began to filter through the curtains. A familiar ache pounded in her temples.

"My migraine is attacking me again," she sighed.

Summoning the strength to face the day, Kring rose, opening her room to confront the reality of a new day. Switching on the dining area lights, she proceeded towards the bathroom, her mind preoccupied with the tasks ahead. However, as she swung the door open, an unexpected sight awaited her. Her husband lay unconscious on the floor, a small pool of blood staining the pristine surface. Concern mingled with irritation as she attempted to rouse him.

"Hey Jose! Wake up! Why are you sleeping here?" Her husband remained unresponsive.

"I don't care! If you don't get up, stay there forever!" Kring declared, frustration and fatigue evident in her voice.

The pressing demands of the day beckoned her, and with a stern resolve, she grabbed her footstool and rattan basket, closing the front door behind her as she ventured into the morning.

By 7 o'clock in the morning, Jay, emerged from his room. Intent on his morning routine, he made his way to the bathroom. Returning to his room, he noticed his father still lying on the floor. Concern etched on the young man's face, he gently tapped his father's back, unaware of the complexities that lingered beneath the seemingly ordinary surface of their lives.

"Hey, Pa! Wake up!"

Jay's urgent plea echoed through the room as he entered, breaking the stillness of the moment.

Confusion etched across his face as he noticed his father holding a bottle of fish sauce with an unusual grip. Without hesitation, he gently took the bottle from his father's hand, placing it aside.

A sudden realization hit him like a wave crashing on the shore. Jay's eyes widened as he observed his father's fingers, now tinged with an unsettling shade of gray. Alarmed, he swiftly grabbed his father's shoulder, attempting to reposition him into a supine position. It was then that the gravity of the situation became undeniable.

"Oh, God! My father is not breathing!"

Panic set in as Jay grappled with the reality before him. Swiftly deciding on the need for assistance, he rushed outside, his pounding heart driving him to knock on the door of their neighbor, Tina. The door creaked open, revealing a young and skinny figure in tight shorts.

"Oh! It's you, Jay!"

Tina's casual greeting contrasted sharply with Jay's distressed demeanor. He struggled to convey the severity of the situation.

"My father is not oo…okay," Jay stammered, his words stumbling in his haste.

"He's not breathing and unresponsive."

Determined to act swiftly, Tina offered a solution. "Call a tricycle to bring him to the hospital.

Go to Ben's house! He has a trike!" Jackie instructed.

Without hesitation, Jay darted towards Ben's residence, his footsteps quick and urgent. In a matter of minutes, both Ben and Jay returned, ready to assist. They carefully picked up Jose, situating him inside the waiting tricycle.

"Come on, let's go to the nearest hospital!" yelled Jay.

The trike sped through the streets, racing against time to reach the hospital. Tension ran high as the trio navigated the city's night, their destination fixed in their minds. After a brief but agonizing journey, they reached the hospital's entrance.

A security guard guided them toward the emergency room, their desperate faces illuminated by the harsh hospital lights. The ER nurses sprang into action, swiftly bringing a stretcher to transfer Jose inside.

"Where is the doctor?" Jay's voice quivered with a mix of anxiety and urgency.

"Relax, sir! Another nurse is calling the doctor on duty," the guard reassured.

A tall, skinny figure in a white gown emerged from his quarters, capturing Jay's attention. As the doctor approached, Jay couldn't help but feel a sense of familiarity.

"His face and height resemble a TV personality I know, but I forget the name," Jay mumbled to himself, a fleeting distraction from the gravity of the situation unfolding in the emergency room.

The doctor approached the lifeless body with a solemn air, his steps measured as he prepared to deliver the grave news. With a stethoscope draped around his neck, he placed the diaphragm on the chest, the act of auscultation resonating through the hushed air of the emergency room. The room held its breath as the doctor, with precision, opened one eye and then the other, shining a penlight to discern any signs of life.

"Who is the relative of the patient?" the doctor inquired, breaking the heavy silence.

"I am, doctor!" Jay's voice trembled as he stepped forward.

The doctor's gaze shifted toward Jay, delivering the news with a gravity that echoed in the sterile atmosphere. "Your father has no heartbeat. He's been dead for several hours now. We cannot do anything to revive him."

The weight of the words hung in the air, and Jay, overwhelmed, covered his face. "I will get my mother."

"I'm really sorry that you had to witness what had happened to your father," the doctor placed his hand on Jay's shoulder.

An hour later, Jay returned with his mother Kring and sister in tow. The family entered the ER, their footsteps echoing a mournful cadence. The doctor, now a bearer of condolences, approached them with a sympathetic demeanor.

"I am sorry for your loss," he expressed, his words laden with genuine empathy.

Kring struggled to control her sobs as the flood of emotions threatened to engulf her. Amidst the grief, a sudden flashback transported her to the turbulent days when Jose's actions inflicted pain upon their family. She recalled the times he returned home intoxicated, resorting to physical abuse when his expectations weren't met.

Most vividly, she remembered the verbal onslaughts and the times he lashed out in anger, leaving her physically battered. In the hushed corridors of the hospital, her voice barely above a whisper, Kring addressed the memory of the departed.

"You gave me too much headache. I did not report you to the authorities because I wanted our family intact. And now you are dead," Kring mumbled, the bitterness of the past interwoven with the sorrow of the present.

Turning her attention to the practicalities, Kring engaged with the ER nurse, discussing the intricate details of the funeral process. With a resolute decision, she expressed her desire for the wake to be held in the sanctity of their home.

As the family grappled with the harsh reality of their loss, the funeral service arrived at the ER, its solemn presence signaling the beginning of the somber journey to bid farewell to Jose's departed soul.

THE WAKE

Under the overcast sky, Jay toiled with determination, hammering nails into the makeshift tent that stood sentinel on the front side of their house. A pole rose to meet the clouds, a sturdy emblem of a communal effort. He paused for a moment, sweat glistening on his forehead, and expressed his gratitude.

"Thanks to the mayor for renting this tent out for us," he acknowledged, a flicker of appreciation in his tired eyes.

Jasmin, alongside her mother, fervently arranged chairs and tables, creating a space where the impending visitors could share their condolences. A small oasis of solace amid the storm of emotions.

"Yes! The good thing is that they have things like this for people like us," Jasmin remarked, her words carrying a mixture of gratitude and resilience.

As the sun dipped below the horizon, casting shadows upon their preparations, Kring gathered her children, a brief respite from their labor.

"Kids! Let's go inside and eat. I know you are all hungry. Anyway, we are almost done," she declared, her voice a soothing melody amid the chaos.

"I will prepare the food, Ma, and clean the dishes," Jasmin volunteered, her determination matching the weight of her grief.

"Where is Joey?" Jasmin inquired, a trace of concern woven into her words.

"I don't know!" Jay replied, his gaze shifting towards the distance.

Time crawled with a quiet agony, and the stillness was pierced by the distant barking of their dogs. Jay's instincts kicked in, and he hurried to the door, hoping for a sign of the approaching funeral service.

"Ma! Here comes the funeral service," he exclaimed, rushing to the gate and swinging it open to welcome the somber procession.

The casket, a vessel carrying the weight of final goodbyes, found its resting place beneath the open tent.

Faces hushed in reverence as the shroud covering Jose's visage was gently lifted, allowing the mourners a last glimpse.

Suddenly, Joey, the elusive presence, entered through the side door of their house. Kring's anger surged, demanding answers.

"Where have you been?" she asked, her tone laced with frustration.

"It is not this time to answer your question, Ma!" Joey asserted, grabbing some leftover food and settling into the dining area.

Kring, her arm draped protectively across her belly, fixed her gaze on him. The air held tension, a silent exchange of unspoken words.

After finishing his meal, Joey informed his mother, "I'll be back, Ma!" A purposeful stride led him to his father's casket, a private communion with the departed.

He walked away, leaving Jay and Jasmin frozen, their emotions caught in the undertow of conflicting sentiments. People, arriving from different corners of the town, offered condolences, their collective presence forming a tapestry of shared grief.

Pedring, a known mahjong player in town, approached Jay, his request for a table revealing the delicate balance between life's routine and the gravity of the moment.

In a corner, beneath the looming shadow of grief, a table was set up—a gathering point for gamblers immersed in their games and the curious onlookers who had come to witness the spectacle. The air hung heavy with the scent of cigarettes and the muted chatter of those seeking solace in the mundane routine of cards.

Amidst this solemn tableau, Leila's family approached, the tendrils of condolences reaching out from one heart to another.

"Deep sympathy to you and your family, Kring," Leila expressed, her words laced with genuine empathy.

"Thank you! Come on, have a seat," Kring responded, gesturing towards the makeshift gathering.

Leila, her curiosity piqued by the abrupt shift in the narrative, sought answers. "What happened?

Yesterday, we were just peddling in the market, and now, it's a different story," she inquired.

Kring, her voice tinged with the weight of recent events, recounted the abrupt and tragic turn of Jose's fate.

"I saw him lying on the floor. I thought he was just sleeping because he was drunk. I changed my shirt and then hurried up for the market. After several hours, Jay came and told me that Jose was in the hospital ER and dead. The doctor told me that he had been dead for several hours before he got into the ER. That's what happened."

Leila, with a wisdom that transcended the moment, offered words of comfort. "Sorry to hear that! We know that Jose's time has come. Every person here on earth has their own time. We have our time coming. So, we must be prepared."

Reflecting on the complexities of life, Leila continued, "You know, Leila, I still remember the days when he was kind to me when he was still courting me, got married, and until he lost his job. Jose joined his alcoholic friends. In fact, five years ago, he consulted his doctor because he was found out to have starting liver cirrhosis due to his alcoholism. His doctor wanted him to cease his liquor drinking habit, but he was stubborn.

That's life, Kring. There are always opposites here on earth. If you are good, there's bad. If you are gorgeous, there is ugly."

"You are right, Leila," Kring acknowledged, her gaze distant, lost in the memories of a life that now belonged to the past.

As the exchanges of life's profound truths unfolded, Kring's attention shifted to a friend at the gate.

"Jay! Please meet Tacio at the gate!" she called out.

"Okay, Ma!"

"Mr. Tacio! How are you doing?" Jay greeted, the ebb and flow of life continuing, even in the shadow of death.

The atmosphere inside the modest abode shifted as Mr. Tacio, a seasoned visitor, was welcomed into the somber space.

"Please come inside!"

"Oh! You have several visitors."

"Please sit here, sir. Would you like something to drink, sir?"

Politeness lingered in the air, but Mr. Tacio, declining the offer, requested a more personal connection.

"No, Jay, thanks! Just sit beside me."

The room, now a theater for life's unfolding drama, awaited the revelation that Mr. Tacio had brought with him.

"Do you know that your father is talented?" he inquired, his words carrying a touch of nostalgia.

"I did not know that, sir," Jay replied, his curiosity piqued.

"Jose had a good voice, and he also used to play the guitar. He sometimes sang and played in our drinking sessions," Mr. Tacio revealed, a glimpse into a side of Jose that had remained hidden from his family.

"Really?" Jay responded, a mix of surprise and regret in his voice.

"Yes! It is true, Jay."

"Had I learned that then, I should have told him to join a singing contest. But now, it's too late," Jay mused. Mr. Tacio's laughter filled the room briefly.

Mr. Tacio, his tone turning somber, continued, "Yes, it is so sad, Jay, that he just wasted his life into alcoholism and ended his life that way. Your father slowly killed himself. I accept that I am drinking alcohol, but it is not habitual. We are giving Jose advice to stop drinking too much liquor, to go home and help your family. He loved his other friends who also love alcohol. Instead of doing good for himself and the family, he listened to the bad effects of alcoholism. You know what I mean, kid."

"Yes, Mr. Tacio!" Jay acknowledged, the weight of realization settling in his young heart.

"When is the burial?" Mr. Tacio inquired, shifting the conversation to the impending farewell.

"On the third day, sir."

"Okay! I have to see your father, then I will go home. Oh! I have to meet your mom too."

"Kid, be good always!"

"Thank you, Mr. Tacio!" Jay expressed gratitude, the layers of complexity in life unraveling within the confines of their home.

Brawl in the Wake

The second day of the wake lingered in the shadow of grief, an unrelenting parade of mourners paying their respects. Amidst the somber air, Gina, a sister to the departed Jose, emerged with her family in tow, having traveled from a distant province. Kring, ever the gracious host, extended warm hospitality to the newly arrived guests.

"It's been far too long since our paths crossed," Gina remarked, embracing her bereaved brother's family and neighbors. A weighty silence enveloped the room as they settled into a conversation that navigated the intricate tapestry of their shared history.

"How is life in your corner of the world?" Gina inquired with a genuine concern that cut through the polite formalities.

"It's been hard," admitted Jose's friend, echoing the sentiment that had become a refrain in their conversations. Gina nodded knowingly, drawing parallels between her brother and an uncle who, once slipping into the abyss of inactivity, found escape in the refuge of laziness.

"He resisted the call to a more diligent life," Gina sighed, her eyes reflecting on the struggle she had witnessed in her brother. "I tried pushing him towards a job, but it only led to heated arguments."

"You've hit the nail on the head, Gina. He lashed out when faced with the prospect of effort," agreed the sympathetic friend.

Their contemplative exchange was abruptly shattered by a commotion emanating from the mahjong table. Raul's voice cut through the air like a discordant note, demanding the prize he believed he had earned.

"I won this game, Pedring! Hand over my prize!" Raul's voice, laden with impatience, reverberated through the room.

"No, you didn't win! The prize is earned, not demanded!" Pedring's obstinate response only fueled Raul's anger.

The dispute escalated, and the room quivered with tension. In an unsettling twist, Pedring's hand slipped to the concealed recesses of his jeans, retrieving a gun. The gasps of onlookers harmonized with the metallic click as the weapon was brandished, aimed menacingly at Raul.

A brief brawl happened then a deafening sound of a gunshot reverberated through the room, momentarily eclipsing the gravity of the moment. Raul, seizing the chaos, bolted from the scene, leaving Pedring sprawled on the floor, a macabre tableau of blood staining the ground beneath him.

A collective gasp surged through the room, followed by urgent pleas for help. Amid the chaos, one spectator, grappling with the reality of the violence that had unfolded, mused, "People are becoming hotheaded nowadays."

The police arrived swiftly, casting a net of interrogation over the eyewitnesses. An ambulance, its siren cutting through the night, carried Pedring's limp form to the nearest hospital. The aftermath lingered, leaving the mourners with a chilling reminder of how easily desperation could ignite into lethal flames.

"It's just money," a spectator murmured in disbelief, contemplating the senseless violence that had shattered the solemnity of the wake. "Why resort to a gun for the sake of money?" The question lingered in the air, a haunting refrain in a world where the pursuit of prize could turn deadly.

Kring was shocked. There was a lot of noise behind her, and it broke the quiet and serious atmosphere. It felt like a big disrespect.

"That person didn't care about this place," Kring said, sounding upset.

"It's really scary," Gina added, also surprised.

"It happens everywhere. The sad thing is that it's happening during Jose's wake," Kring said, looking at the unfolding drama.

In the chaos, Kring noticed a lady with a baby who seemed interested in Jose's face. Kring went up to her to find out more.

"May I know your name, ma'am?" Kring asked politely.

The lady took off her sunglasses. "I'm Lovely, Jose's girlfriend. And you?" she said.

"I'm Kring, Jose's wife," Kring replied, feeling tense.

There was a tense moment between them, and Kring couldn't hold back her emotions. She pushed away Lovely, who then gave her son to someone else as things got worse.

People watched, but no one stepped in as the two women fought. It got so intense that they accidentally knocked over the coffin.

The coffin fell, and the cover came off, revealing Jose's body.

Seeing Jose like that made the fight stop. Kring told Lovely to leave, and she did, holding her son.

Some kind people came forward and helped fix the situation. They put Jose back in the coffin.

On the third day, more than fifty people came for the funeral. They walked to the cemetery and watched as Jose was laid to rest in the ground.

As the last bits of dirt fell, Kring, surrounded by friends, said thank you. With tears in her eyes, she said her final goodbye to her husband. It was a sad farewell, with unexpected trouble at the wake.

JAIL

After enduring several exhausting days, Kring rouses herself from a fitful slumber around 8 o'clock in the morning. The weariness lingers in her eyes, etched deep into the lines of her face. Shaking off the remnants of sleep, she ventures out of her room and proceeds to knock on Joey's door.

There is no response.

Undeterred, Kring takes it upon herself to swing the door open. Frustration and concern etch lines on her face as she confronts her reclusive son.

"Hey! Why won't you open the door? Why did you skip your father's funeral? And why are you holed up in here all the time, avoiding everyone?" Kring's questions spill forth, laden with a mix of exasperation and worry.

"Ma, can you just let me be? I don't need you interrogating me about everything. I'm not a child anymore! Now, please, leave me alone and close the door. I need some time alone!" Joey retorts, his frustration echoing through his words.

"Fine! But show some courtesy, will you?" Kring retorts, slamming the door shut with a resounding bang.

"Why does he always lock himself away?" Kring mutters to herself, a gnawing sense of unease settling within her.

"I sense that he's hiding. He's concealing something. Something that might be unacceptable to me or to others. Yes, that's it. I need to find out the truth," she resolves, her determination taking root.

"I'll talk to his friends. I'll call them later. But first, I have to go to the market and earn some money," she decides, closing the doors of her house behind her as she embarks on a mission to uncover the mystery shrouding her son.

In the bustling market, as she arranges her makeshift stall, Kring is greeted by Leila.

"Hello, Kring! How are you?" Leila chirps.

"I'm good! Here we are again, by the side of this public market, sidewalk vending," Kring replies, her words punctuated by the resilient spirit that drives her forward.

"You're absolutely right, Kring!" Leila concurs, and together, they navigate the challenges of their daily grind along the bustling roadside market.

"Hey madam! Tomatoes? My veggies are fresh!" Kring's voice carried through the air, reaching out to passing customers in the lively market.

"How much per kilo for your tomatoes?" inquired a curious customer.

"Thirty pesos," replied Kring with a welcoming smile.

"Give me three kilos, please," the customer decided.

"Alright, madam! Pick your desired tomatoes and place them on this steel plate, and I'll weigh them for you."

"Okay! Here are your tomatoes, madam!"

The transaction concluded smoothly, and the customer handed over the payment. "Thank you, madam!

Please come again!" Kring expressed her gratitude.

"You're welcome! Yes, I will," the customer replied, fading into the market crowd.

"I saw that, Kring," Leila remarked, acknowledging Kring's successful sale.

"By the way, can I borrow your mobile phone, Leila?" Kring requested.

"Why?" Leila asked.

"I need to call Molly. He's Joey's best friend."

"Is there anything wrong?"

"I want to unravel the mystery surrounding my son. This is the first time I've noticed him acting this way—keeping himself away from people. He's been confined to his room all day and didn't help entertain visitors during his father's wake. He didn't even attend his father's funeral."

"Okay, here's the phone. Do you have Molly's contact number?"

"Yes, he gave me his number when he and his friend visited our house," Kring said in deep thought as she shifted between reading her notebook and pressing the keypad.

"Hello! Is this Molly?" Kring inquired once connected.

"Yes, this is Molly."

"This is Kring, Joey's mother. Do you have an idea what is happening to Joey? My son seems unusually quiet these past few days. Where is he now?" Kring probed, a hint of concern in her voice.

The weight of uncertainty hung heavily in the air as Kring processed the revelation from Molly. He had been inside their house for quite some time, a revelation that left Kring and Leila in an uneasy silence.

"Okay, ma'am! We will meet him. Bye!" Molly's parting words resonated through the air as the connection ended.

"Hello! Hello, Molly!" Kring called out desperately, her voice echoing in the emptiness that followed.

Leila observed her with a concerned look. "So, what did Molly say?" she inquired, breaking the silence.

"He didn't answer my question directly. He just said he will meet Joey in our house," Kring replied with a heavy sigh.

"Let's get back to work," Kring proclaimed, the weight of the unknown settling heavily on her shoulders.

With a sudden burst of energy, Kring took to the streets, hawking her vegetables. "Hey, madam! Buy my veggies. They're all fresh. It's cheaper now. I want to go home early," she called out, her words a blend of desperation and determination.

Leila, taken aback, questioned, "What are these words about going home early?"

"Yes, I want to… because I feel something different about my son," Kring confessed, the urgency in her voice palpable.

Leila checked the time and responded, "It's 4:30 PM."

"Okay! Please sell my remaining veggies and just give my principal amount. And, please keep my things," Kring instructed abruptly.

"What?" Leila reacted, bewildered.

Ignoring the question, Kring hurriedly walked away, her steps quickening into a run as she raced back home.

Upon her return, a sense of foreboding gripped her as she noticed the gate and front door wide open.

Panic and fear surged through her veins.

"Oh my goodness! Why are there shirts scattered on the floor? Why has Joey's door been smashed?"

Kring's mind buzzed with a multitude of questions.

She fought the urge to scream and opted for control.

"I should go to my neighbor," she mumbled to herself.

"Hey, Manny! Did you see my son?" she asked, her voice shaky.

"Yes, Kring! He was handcuffed by four policemen," Manny replied solemnly.

A wave of shock and sorrow washed over Kring. She held back tears, expressing gratitude to Manny.

"Thank you, Manny! I will go to the police station," she declared with determination, her heart heavy with the looming unknown.

THE REVELATION

Kring stepped into the stark surroundings of the police station, a place she never thought she'd find herself in. Her eyes darted around the room, scanning the faces of officers and the muted chatter of those waiting. Determination etched her features as she approached the front desk.

"Where is my son, sir? Where did you put him?" Kring inquired, her voice edged with worry.

"What is his name?" the officer at the front desk asked.

"Joey, sir," Kring replied, her anxiety palpable.

The officer checked the name lists. "He is under investigation in the second room. Have a seat first on the corner bench over there. Someone will call you."

"No…no, I am disturbed now and anxious. I cannot sit," Kring declared, pacing starting to and from the desk.

"Hey, lady!" called an officer.

Kring turned her head towards the calling officer. "Madam, the investigation is done. Your son is inside cell number 2 now. I will guide you there. Come on, let's go!"

As they approached the cell, Kring's heart raced. "Please let him out," she pleaded, desperation tinging her voice.

"Hey, lady! What is your name?" the officer asked.

"Kring, officer."

"Kring, you have to go and find a lawyer for your son."

"Why should I find a lawyer? I don't understand. My son is kind. He could never do anything illegal!"

Kring's voice trembled with disbelief.

The officer sighed, "Your son was involved in a homicide with rape. There is a public attorney's office to help you. Go to the front desk, and they will guide you."

"Okay, but can I talk to my son first?" Kring implored, her eyes searching for any sign of reassurance.

Kring, her heart heavy with both disbelief and dread, approached the room where Joey lay on the bed.

"Hey, Joey! My son!" she called out, her voice tinged with a mixture of concern and desperation.

Joey lay motionless on the bed, his gaze fixed on the ceiling. It was as if he didn't hear the anguished words pouring from his mother's mouth. The weight of the room mirrored the weight in Kring's heart.

In a moment of painful revelation, Joey began to recount the horrifying events that transpired. "I was drinking liquor with Russel and Molly. We were just having fun at Molly's house. We finished that drinking spree around 2 AM. We didn't have enough money, but Russel wanted to drink more, so we decided to randomly rob a house."

His eyes remained distant as he continued his chilling narrative.

"We were walking quietly along the alley when we spotted a young lady dressing up in her room. Her window was open and just covered by a transparent curtain. The house was a bungalow. We broke into the slightly opened window in the kitchen and went straight to the lady's room."

Joey's voice trembled as he detailed the horrifying scene.

"The young beautiful lady was sitting in front of the dresser, combing her hair. She wore a nightdress and no bra. She yelled when she saw us. Russel covered her mouth and dragged her to bed. Molly was holding her legs."

Joey continued to recount the events in his mind.

"Hey, Joey," Russel commanded, "close the window and cover it with a thick curtain. Come up here to hold her other arm."

"Okay!" Joey replied mechanically.

Molly pulled up the long shirt and took down the panties.

The horrifying truth unfolded in Joey's mind, "The beautiful and sexy body of the lady was exposed. Molly raped her first. Russel was next, and I was the last. They told me to strangle her.

Then, we ransacked the house, taking a mobile phone, laptop, cash, and jewelry."

The chilling confession lingered in the air as Kring, devastated, pleaded with her son.

"Hey, Joey, answer me!"

"He's not responding. Go back tomorrow," the officer suggested, his voice carrying the weight of the situation.

"Yes, you're right. Maybe he's tired now," Kring whispered, her voice breaking.

Seeking solace and assistance, Kring approached the front desk officer, inquiring about attorney services.

After gathering information, she departed the police station, her mind and heart entangled in a web of emotions and unimaginable truths.

THE STROKE

Kring slouched on a worn-out bench, the dull facade of the police station looming over her. Her demeanor mirrored the desolation of a lost soul, and her eyes betrayed the turmoil within. A gust of wind played with loose strands of her hair as she mumbled, almost inaudibly, "I will go to Jasmin and tell her what is happening to his brother."

As she ambled along the roadside, the merciless sun beat down on her, its searing rays seemingly irrelevant to her existence. Unmindful of the rivulets of sweat tracing paths down her face and body, Kring trudged forward, her mind seemingly emptied of any coherent thoughts.

"One kilometer more to reach Jasmin," she murmured to herself, a mantra against the weight of her own despair.

The pain in her right heel, a relentless companion, resurfaced, prompting her to seek refuge on the roadside. Sitting on the dusty ground, she gingerly removed her shoe, emitting a soft cry of pain. A bruise, marked with minimal bleeding, marred her heel.

"It is too achy," she admitted to the empty air, her wristwatch revealing the passage of time: 5:30 PM.

"I have to put this shoe back on and walk again," she muttered, urgency replacing self-pity as darkness descended. Forty arduous minutes later, Kring arrived at her destination – her daughter Jasmin's house.

The dog behind the gate announced her arrival with a cacophony of barks.

"Jasmin! I am afraid of your dog," Kring exclaimed as her daughter approached the gate, her face etched with concern.

"Ma!" Jasmin replied, ushering her in, "What are you doing here at this time? It's dusky now! Come inside."

"Wait, Ma! I have to remove the clothes from the couch," Jasmin continued, bustling about.

Observing her surroundings, Kring acquiesced, "Okay! You can sit now, Ma. I will prepare your dinner. I know you haven't had dinner yet."

Ever the caretaker, Kring offered, "I will help you, Jasmin."

"No, Ma! Just sit and watch TV," Jasmin insisted, preparing a plate of rice and vegetables for her mother.

As Kring hesitated, Jasmin queried, "What is the reason for your coming here at this hour, Ma?" The air in the cramped apartment hung heavy with unspoken words, the answer to that question looming like a storm on the horizon.

"Your brother Joey is in jail now," Kring solemnly declared, her words hanging heavy in the air.

"What, Ma? How did it happen?" Jasmin's eyes widened with shock and concern.

"I...I do not know," Kring replied, her voice tinged with helplessness. "I will go back there tomorrow to talk with Joey. Please visit your brother too," Kring urged.

"I will try, Ma."

"Okay! Thanks for the food. I like it!"

"Thanks, Ma!"

"I have to go now," Kring announced, preparing to leave. Jasmin, sensing her mother's dire situation, reached into her left shorts pocket and handed her some money.

"Here, Ma! Accept this cash. Ride public transport. Don't walk, you must be tired now!"

"Thank you for this! Actually, I have bleeding callus on my heel," Kring explained, her voice a mixture of gratitude and pain. She embraced Jasmin tightly, whispering, "I love you!" as tears welled up in her eyes.

"Okay, I am leaving now," Kring said, breaking the hug but carrying the weight of her worries with her.

The following morning found Kring back at the police station. The officer summoned Joey, and between the cold bars, mother and son engaged in a desperate conversation.

"Ma! Please find a way to get me out from here," Joey pleaded.

"You know, son, we do not have money to pay for the lawyer and parole," Kring admitted, a heavy sigh escaping her lips.

"It is Molly who is the mastermind of this trouble. I do not understand how I am the only one here," Joey explained, unraveling a sinister plot.

Kring suddenly experienced a severe headache, the pain throbbing through her temples.

"What happened, Ma? Why are you holding your head? Speak up!" Joey urged, concern etched on his face.

"I always experience this headache," Kring said, massaging her forehead and temples as her eyes closed, the weight of the situation pressing upon her.

"I love my children. This is my worst headache in life," she admitted, her words echoing with the ache of a mother caught in the storm of her children's misdeeds.

The air in the room hung heavy with tension as heaving sounds filled the space—Joey doubled over, unable to contain the contents of his stomach. The harsh reality of the situation hit him like a tidal wave, and the unsettling symphony of retching echoed through the sterile walls.

Then, in an instant, the focus shifted. She, the matriarch, crumpled like a puppet with severed strings, collapsing onto the unforgiving floor. Panic set in, and Joey's voice pierced the chaos, desperate and raw, "Help...help, officer! Please help my mother!"

Responding to the urgent plea, police officers rushed to the scene, lifting the unconscious figure of Kring and carrying her, a fragile burden, to the car and onto the nearest hospital. The emergency room became a stage for a different kind of drama, one that unfolded within the confines of life and death.

The doctor, with a sense of urgency, examined Kring. A silent gravity filled the room as the doctor observed her limp limbs devoid of reflex and noted the alarming blood pressure reading of 220/110.

"Where are the relatives of the patient, officer?" the doctor inquired.

"He is the mother of our prisoner," the officer explained, his words hanging in the charged atmosphere.

"We'll go back to the police station and ask the prisoner about the names of their immediate family."

"We are in an emergency situation, and we have to do a CT scan right now."

"Do the procedure now, doctor," an officer replied.

"But we have some papers to sign," the doctor hesitated.

"I know what you mean, doctor. Since this is an emergency, we will take care of the first expense of the scan."

"Okay, we'll do it."

"Can we leave now, doctor?"

"Please give us your contact number so that we can update the relatives through you."

"Ok! Here, doctor."

After a few minutes, the CT scan results materialized in the doctor's hands, revealing a grim diagnosis—hemorrhagic stroke, specifically subarachnoid hemorrhage. The urgency intensified as the nurse was summoned to convey a message to the waiting police officers.

"Nurse, please call the police officer and tell them to inform the relatives to come here as soon as possible. Thank you!"

Hours passed like an agonizing eternity until Jasmin and Jay, faces etched with worry, arrived at the emergency room. Their eyes sought answers from the attending doctor.

"Doctor, what is the status of our mom?" Jasmin inquired, her voice quivering.

"Your mom is comatose now. There is too much blood that accumulated in her brain. We need to refer her to the neurosurgeon as soon as possible." The stark truth hung in the air, leaving the family grappling with the uncertain journey that lay ahead.

The weight of the words hung heavily in the sterile hospital room. Jasmin, her eyes red from tears, mustered the courage to voice their grim reality, "We do not have money for that procedure, doctor."

Unexpectedly, the cardiac monitor's alarms shattered the heavy silence, jolting the room into a frenzied urgency. The doctor, apologetic but resolute, addressed the distraught siblings,

"There is an emergency with your mom now. Will you excuse us?"

Helplessly, Jasmin and Jay watched from a distance as the medical staff hurriedly engaged in a desperate move to revive their mother. The rhythmic compressions of CPR echoed in the room, drowning out the siblings' anguished silence. They found solace on a nearby couch, where Jasmin, overcome with grief, let her tears flow freely. Jay, a pillar of strength in the face of tragedy, consoled his sister with silent understanding.

The doctor, emerging from behind the curtain, walked towards the siblings. The weight of sorrow etched on his face, he sat beside them and gently uttered the words that would alter the course of their lives, "I am sorry. We did everything to revive your mom. But she passed away."

The world seemed to halt as the siblings absorbed the crushing reality of their mother's demise. The hospital staff orchestrated the somber procession of the funeral service, gently taking Kring's lifeless body away from the now-hushed room.

In the wake of their mother's passing, Jasmin and Jay made the difficult decision to visit Joey and share the heart-wrenching news. The prison walls couldn't contain the waves of grief as they all cried together, a family shattered by the cruel hand of fate.

"We will go home now, Joey. We will prepare everything for Mom's wake," Jay assured his incarcerated brother, a heavy burden of responsibility settling on his shoulders.

Joey, confined within the cold walls of his cell, faced the torment of self-blame. "I am very sorry, Mom. I know I am the cause of your death," he whispered to himself, the weight of guilt piercing through his tears. Inside the prison's solitude, a son mourned the irreversible consequences of his actions, the echoes of remorse reverberating in the emptiness of his confinement.

www.ingramcontent.com/pod-product-compliance
Lightning Source LLC
LaVergne TN
LVHW051225070526
838200LV00057B/4615